# AMY LEE AND THE DARKNESS HEX

WRITTEN BY AMY LEE

SCHOLASTIC

Scholastic Children's Books
An imprint of Scholastic Ltd
Euston House, 24 Eversholt Street, London, NW1 1DB, UK
Registered office: Westfield Road, Southam, Warwickshire, CV47 0RA


First published in the UK by Scholastic Ltd, 2017



ISBN 978 1407 17223 1

A CIP catalogue record for this book
is available from the British Library.



Printed by CPI Group (UK) Ltd, Croydon, CR0 4YY
Papers used by Scholastic Children's Books are made
from wood grown in sustainable forests.

5 7 9 10 8 6



www.scholastic.co.uk

**I dedicate this book to my mum. Love you.**

**And huge thanks to Lilly Ladjevardi for all of her support on this book!**

# CHAPTER 1

Captain Silverbeard swings his mighty golden sword in my direction.

"Give up the treasure, old grey beard!" I shout, taking cover behind the crow's nest pole.

"Grey beard?" The burly captain stops mid-swing of his cutlass. "My beard is silver, not grey! It's distinguished! Arrrh!"

I chuckle to myself: age has always been the pirate's weakness. The swaying ship helps me to roll to the right, and I am on guard with my pink jewelled sword. "That gold doesn't belong to you, old man! It belongs to the town of Driftwood Bay!"

Silverbeard's sword almost gets me, but I am too quick, leaping on to the upper deck.

"The treasure belongs to whoever's strong enough to take it," he snarls. "And, princess, that's me! Arrrh!"

We parry, our blades flashing pink and gold in the hot midday sun. But I use my higher position to disarm him at last with one decisive strike of my sword, and his cutlass skitters across the deck and falls off the edge of the ship, disappearing into the crashing waves.

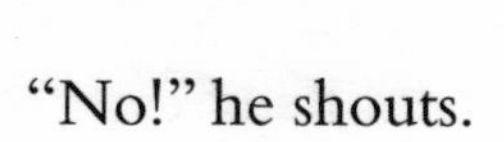

"No!" he shouts.

I jump back down, my sword pointing to his chest.

"Now who's strongest?" I say, cocking an eyebrow. "Looks like I'm not just some delicate little princess, after all. I am a hero!"

The captain barks.

—wait, what? He barks? Like a dog? I knew he was crazy, but barking?

Suddenly, I feel something warm and wet against my cheek. Is it blood? Did he get me?

Captain Silverbeard is fading away, the ship is fading away, the whole world is fading away!

I open my eyes to find Mars licking my face. "Mars! I was this close to beating Captain Silverbeard!"

My heroic dog must have sensed danger and come to my rescue. Even in my dreams.

I sit up and stretch out my arms. "You can't rescue me in my sleep, Mars. It was my chance to prove how strong and brave I can be!" Sometimes it feels like I am always so overprotected.

I stroke Mars's silky ears as his shiny eyes look up at me. I can't stay mad at that little face for too long.

All of a sudden I am under attack with doggy kisses as my bed is invaded by more furry creatures. I try to hide my face under the pillow, but then the dogs start to lick my toes in their morning game of 'Let's Wake Up Amy!'

"OK, OK, I hear ya!" I say, laughing and petting Max, Lexi, Luna, Sailor, Boomer, Lola, Romeo and Destiny in turn. "Wanna hear about my dream? I almost got Captain Silverbeard!"

The nine dogs sit and listen patien

dream. By the end, Max and Mars both have their ta

Anything to do with adventure excites them!

"Well, let's get you guys some breakfast," I say. "How about some fish?"

The dogs whimper in response, and I laugh at the unimpressed expressions on their faces.

OK, how about some nice

pack are jumping up and down

Ha, ha! OK, guys, let me go grab you some!"

I leave my bedroom and bump into Bert, an iron golem who lives with me. He's a huge man made of metal, and he's normally very friendly, but right now he doesn't even notice me.

"Good morning, Bert!"

He still doesn't acknowledge me. Bert's nose is almost touching the oak wood blocks that decorate my home.

"OK, Bert, enjoy the block of the day!" I'm not mad at his manners; he just loves those blocks! Every morning he chooses a new one to love, and he gets lost in his own little world. And I know a thing or two about getting distracted by daydreams…

In the kitchen, I can see my other iron golem looking out the window. "Bertha! Good morning!"

Upon hearing my voice, Bertha turns around, excited. But she looks straight over my head.

"Bertha, I'm right here sweetie, remember? Look down!" I try to remind her, jumping up and down.

She turns around and heads towards the dining room.

"No, Bertha! Behind you! You just have to look past your nose!"

Bertha finally finds me after she tilts her head down. You see, Bertha's nose is so big that I am sometimes out of view for her. I give her a big hug.

"Now, why did I come down here?" I ask myself. "Oh, yeah, I gotta feed those poochies!" I grab a bunch of steak and fish from the refrigerator and head back upstairs. The cats are now awake, and I give them their breakfast of red salmon. Saturn, Comet and Star looove salmon! The dogs wait patiently with their tails wagging as I feed them each a steak in turn and give them all a pat on the head. "Good doggies!"

As the animals attack their meals, I pull on my diamond boots, adjust my tiara and go outside to my balcony, which

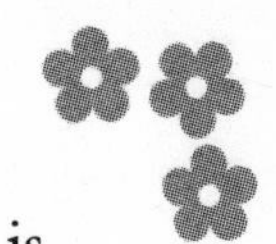

overlooks the Land of Love. Such peacefulness! The sun is shining and the flowers are blooming. I can see Peace Pig and Peace Chicken wandering around the Garden of Peace and Love, cheerfully nosing at brightly coloured flowers. Far off in the distance, tall, stately mountains rise high into the clouds.

Looking out, it's hard to believe that at night-time the beasties wander the land. It's almost like two worlds: my wonderful world in the day, and theirs at night. Two worlds that should never meet.

Everything looks so happy and full of life today, all except for that purple cloud in the distance behind us. Oh, I hope it doesn't rain! I have lots to do!

I was thinking today would be the perfect day to start building my dogs an epic doghouse. They already have a play park, but I really want to build them a house. It could be inside a giant kennel, and it would have slides and treat dispensers and a whole sandbox for digging! Ooh, there could even be flags! Nine of them, in different colours to represent each of my dogs. And there could be bridges connecting several towers, and then I could climb it, and we could play hide and seek, and I could—

I shake my head. *Amy!* I tell myself, ***this isn't a house for you!***

The dogs are now finished with their breakfast and are staring at me, waiting to find out who will be joining me on today's adventure.

"Sorry, guys, I got carried away again! So, who wants to come with me today?"

All the dogs jump excitedly. I look around at each of them, their eyes shining bright, their tongues wagging, eager to be picked.

"Hmm… How about today we take … Luna!"

Luna, my third dog and the first-ever puppy to be born in my family, jumps in delight.

I bend down to tickle her chin and straighten up her yellow collar.

"Loves it. You guys have fun! We'll be back before you know it!" Luna and I head out into the hallway. "But before we head outside, I better check on Mittens and the gang."

As I approach the Happy Room where my three snow golems live – Mittens, Mr Frost and Blizzard – I can hear nothing but silence.

This worries me. This must mean Mittens is up to no good.

Sure enough, I open the door and

**SPLAT!**

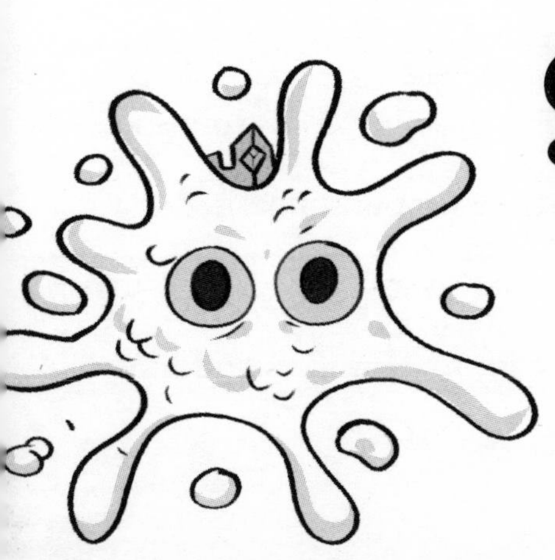

A huge, freezing-cold snowball lands in my face!

“Mittens!” I screech, wiping the snow from my eyes. A catapult has been rigged up to the door. Actually, it’s a pretty cool catapult. Oooooh, maybe I could make a giant version of it on the roof, to fling tasty treats to Peace Pig in the Garden of Peace and Love! Or I could—

I hear Luna bark and look behind me to see Mittens trying to make a getaway. Snow golems are just like traditional snowmen, except with pumpkin helmets, and they glide around looking for mischief. Luckily, Mittens usually leaves a trail of snow, so I can always track him down when he’s wandered off to find some trouble.

“No way, Mittens! You’re not running loose outside today! I have to go out, and I can’t leave you unsupervised all day.”

Although Mittens cannot speak, I can understand him

perfectly. He looks at me with his hollow pumpkin eyes.

"Why? Because you just snowballed me in the face, that's why!"

He makes his eyes as wide as balloons.

"Nope, not falling for it. Don't give me the puppy dog look! It doesn't even work for the dogs! Er, most of the time." I think back and giggle. "Well, it doesn't work for them *some* of the time."

I send him back to his room, then say good morning to Mr Frost and Blizzard. "Please keep Mittens out of trouble!" I call out as I walk Luna towards the supply room.

What a morning! First I get woken up just before a dream victory against my dream nemesis Captain Silverbeard, and then I get snowballed! Let's hope nothing else goes wrong today...

# CHAPTER 2

"Woof!"

Luna is barking excitedly at the front door as she scratches the door frame, eager to get outside.

"I know, I know! I'm coming!" I grab some supplies for today's adventure: food for me and Luna to have a picnic, and a bunch of building supplies.

As soon as I open the front door, Luna almost trips over her paws as she runs over to Grandfather Oak.

My wonderful tree! Grandfather Oak is a magnificent

giant watching over my home. I stare up at him as the sunlight shines through his leafy branches, highlighting all the details of his bark.

"Good morning, Grandfather Oak!"

His wrinkled face smiles down to me, his face welcoming and full of love. I give him a big hug and feel the morning sun on my face. The light twinkles on the surface of the lake nearby, under which I can barely make out huge, friendly squid moving about.

"Good morning, Amy dear."

Although no words are said aloud, Grandfather Oak and I communicate with our inner spirits, one spirit to the other.

"How are you this morning?" I ask as I sit cross-legged in the grass in front of him. Luna gently licks Grandfather Oak before settling in my arms.

The tree chuckles. "Why, thank you, Luna, that was very

kind! Amy, I am having a lovely morning. I saw the sun rise, the birds visited for a morning chat and a young grasshopper told me about his day. How are you?"

"I'm great!" I say eagerly. "I'm excited about my day. I'm going to start building a" – I quickly move my hands to cover up Luna's ears – "huge doggy funhouse. But – shhh! – it's a surprise!"

Grandfather Oak smiles. "That sounds wonderful!"

"Yeah!" I take my hands away from Luna's ears and give them a stroke. "I hope it doesn't rain, though! Check out those dark purple storm clouds over the forest!" I point in the far distance.

Grandfather Oak turns to the direction of the purple clouds. Suddenly, his eyes become very wide. "The dark … the forest…" he mumbles, then becomes very quiet.

I lower my arm as I watch him, confused. After a long moment, I begin to wonder: is my daydreaming catching?

"Grandfather Oak?"

He suddenly breaks from his trance. "Ahem. Yes. Amy, I believe it's time for your story."

"Oh, yes, please!" I stroke Luna's soft, silky ears and edge closer to Grandfather Oak. What will the story be today, I wonder? For as far back as I can remember, every morning Grandfather Oak tells me a brand-new story that he makes up, right on the spot. I treasure those stories, carrying them with me throughout the day. More often than not, the enchanted stories have special meaning for me, such as sound advice for a decision I need to make, or a word of caution about risks I should avoid. Other times, he paints the most incredible pictures in my mind, making my imagination

run in overdrive with mice in space, and friendly sock monsters!

Grandfather Oak closes his eyes and smiles again, although this time his smile seems a bit sadder. He lets out a deep breath. "This is a different kind of story, my dear, from the stories I usually tell you. Like me, it has very deep roots."

Dozens of Grandfather Oak's leaves shiver above me; or is that just a breeze? My arms have goosebumps as I wrap them around Luna.

"Our world is a world of carefully calibrated balance," he continues. "There is day, and there is night. There is goodness, kindness and love," Grandfather Oak pauses to wink at me, "but there is also anger, jealousy and sadness. In daytime we can roam freely and peacefully. The land is ours. But at night, as you know, the land belongs to the dark. It is not safe, and we

must protect ourselves and those we hold dear. This balance is not easy to maintain, and every once in a while someone tips the scales, which leads to chaos for both worlds."

Grandfather Oak takes a moment and simply stares forward. Then he continues in a lower voice. "A long, long time ago there was a young prince who was very kind and just. He had a large family of loyal friends, and every creature – and plant – in the kingdom loved him dearly."

"He sounds a lot like Prince Oliver," I say, dreamily.

Grandfather Oak laughs heartily. "Yes! He does a little, doesn't he? The prince came across a land of darkness, where everything was tainted, even the trees. Everything was full of anger, full of sadness. But the prince was very brave, and he saw what the land could be. He had hope. And hope is a very powerful force. Never forget that, Amy."

I look into his wise eyes and nod.

"With every step the prince took, green grass sprouted in his footsteps, and the light grew, slowly dissolving the darkness. The prince would approach a tree, place his hand upon it and share his energy until the tree's black branches and crispy black leaves would fall. New branches of a healthy sapling would grow from the fallen limbs, spreading goodness right down to the roots."

"Magic," I whisper, my eyes wide as the sun.

Grandfather Oak smiles. "It took a very long time – years and years, in fact. But slowly the land became full of love

and light. One by one, the darkness in the trees, flowers, plants and animals disappeared. The prince married and became king. Soon he had children and taught them how to love and have hope, so that each generation could protect the land."

I smile, imagining royal children running around and playing in this new, happy kingdom.

Then Grandfather Oak's expression suddenly becomes very serious as he continues the story: "But legend has it that not all of the darkness disappeared. That somewhere darkness still grew, waiting for its time to reign once again."

**"KRAAA! KRAAA!"**

A crow's loud call breaks the story's spell. Luna jumps out of my arms and looks around, tail wagging, trying to spot the bird.

"After many years, the king died, and upon his death a

prophecy began, predicting the return of darkness. The king's crown was melted down according to his own instructions. The crown bore three jewels, and each precious gem was placed in the crowns of his three sons, who in turn handed them down to their children, and then their children. The jewels served as a reminder that to overcome darkness, all you need is light. One cannot exist without the other."

I try to hold that thought in my head, rolling it over and feeling its heavy weight. Light and darkness. Day and night. Hope and despair, happiness and sadness.

"Sadly," Grandfather Oak says, "the king's kind heart was not passed down to every member of his family. Some,

curious, dabbled in black magic. Others were jealous that they were not king or queen of the land, and they did more than dabble; they sought vengeance. Consumed by anger, they fulfilled the prophecy and brought despair into the world, tipping the balance of light and dark. They used a powerful curse, a hex of darkness. And, without hope, the land was slowly eaten away by shadows until once again it was a land of evil. The world lay waiting, a wasteland of misery. Then, years later, the king's true successor arrived, and goodness blossomed once again."

Grandfather Oak pauses, and for a second I think he's about to start crying!

But he doesn't. He simply says, "Good can grow from evil, Amy. That's as important a lesson as any I've told."

"That's quite a story, Grandfather Oak," I say uncertainly.

"And a bit sad."

"Sometimes, dear, a little bit of sadness is OK too."

I sit in silence and ponder this for a moment or two. A tiny ladybird crawls along my knee, and I count her spots. Seven! Suddenly, she falls from my leg and lands on the back of her shell in the grass, her little legs dancing away in the air.

"Oh, no!" I bend down and gently lower my pinky finger so the ladybird can climb aboard. She does, then spreads her wings and takes flight, landing on my nose. I giggle.

"That was very kind of you, Amy," Grandfather Oak tells me. "I think she is saying 'thank you'."

I smile as the little ladybird takes flight once more. "Every life deserves a helping hand," I tell him, getting up from the grass. I wave goodbye to Grandfather Oak and wish

him a wonderful rest of the day as Luna and I head towards the bridge that crosses the lake.

"Oh, and Amy," I hear him call out. "Be quick gathering wood in the forest today. I don't like the look of those clouds."

# CHAPTER 3

Just beyond the lake is the Enchanted Treehouse, and directly behind the treehouse lies the desert, vast and wide and full of mysteries. I have already explored one temple here long ago, so I know the desert's secrets are deeper than what you can see on the surface.

Luna playfully runs ahead, sniffing mounds of sand and barking at each cactus, telling them not to hurt me as we pass … or else.

My diamond boots sink slightly in the sand, making the trek across the desert rather tiring. I wonder if I built

snowshoes, would they work in sand? Would they be called sandshoes, then? Oooh, or maybe I could build skis, so I could cross-desert ski? As I ponder these questions, Luna speeds off over a hill of golden sand and disappears from view.

Suddenly I hear a yelp. My heart stops. "Luna?" I shout.

She answers me with a whimper. She's hurt!

I begin to run through the sand, and with each step my boots seem to feel heavier and heavier. Forget skis! I need a snowmobile! Or a helicopter…

At the top of the sand hill I can't see Luna anywhere. I cup my hands around my mouth as I shout, "Luna? Where are you?"

I hear another whimper to my left, where there's a fluffy dog butt sticking out of the sand.

I sigh with relief. "Luna!

I thought you were in real danger!" I gently pull her to safety. Then I notice Luna has actually got stuck in a hole. A hole in the desert?

Luna licks my face in appreciation of her rescue when I bend down to examine the hole. "OK, baby, hold on." It is dark below, but I can see some sort of stone floor. Luna is now intrigued, too, and I have to gently pull her back. "Hmm, what do you think this is, Luna? Another temple? It sure doesn't look like one."

I can make something out... It looks like ... wood? Wooden furniture? I lean forward, my hair now flowing before me. Luna growls, biting my boots in an attempt to pull me back.

Wait! What's that? I see a—

Suddenly I lose my hold and fall down the hole!

AAAAAAAAA AAAAAAAAAAAAAAAAAAAAAAAAAAAAAAAAAAAAAAAAAAAAAAAAAAAAAARRRRRRRRRRRRGHHHH!!!

I land with a thump on the cold stone floor. I hear a bark and look up to see a bunch of fluffy legs flailing above me – just in time to catch Luna!

It doesn't take long for my eyes to adjust to the darkness. Specks of dust fly around me gracefully. It is eerily quiet down here. I hold Luna closer to me, our hearts beating in sync.

Something catches my eye to my right. I jump up and scream,

My feet jump up and down in an awkward dance to keep the snake at bay, and Luna leaps down from my arms and runs straight towards it.

"No, Luna!" I screech. I scramble after her, only to find her wagging her tail, gently nudging the 'snake'.

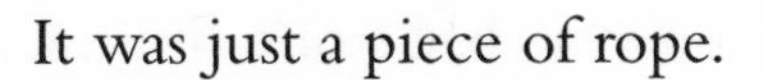

It was just a piece of rope.

I sigh with relief. Why am I such a scaredy-cat all the time? Actually, I bet Saturn, Comet and Star are way braver than I am. Such a scaredy-princess, then? A princess who's only brave in her dreams. I wish I were brave like the prince in Grandfather Oak's story. He saved a whole land from darkness; I get scared in a dark cave with a piece of rope.

A thought suddenly occurs to me: someone must have left that rope here. Maybe they used it to get in and out of the hole! Then I notice markings on the dusty floor. Footprints. Not mine, not Luna's, someone else's.

With shaky hands, I grab my backpack and dig inside for Katniss, my faithful bow.

Oh, no! I forgot to pack it this morning. Without Katniss, I'm defenceless!

I dig around some more and find a torch and some flint and steel. I light the torch, and as the flames make the shadows

of the cave dance, the objects I faintly saw from above come into view.

A bookcase.

Old, musty, dusty leather-bound books pack the shelves.

Curious, I step closer to read the spines: ***Magic for Beginners, White Magic, Powerful Magic, The Dark Powers Within***... The titles of the books become darker in magic as I go along. But there's a gap at the end of the shelf, where the dust has been disturbed. Someone has removed this book.

**"AAAAAAAAAAAAAH!"**

I scream again – but this time because I felt a mouse run across my foot! At least I hope it was a mouse and not a rat! Or worse...

Trembling, I follow the wall further into the gloom. Spiderwebs sway in the cave's draught as a wooden desk comes into view. There's a heavy, leather-bound book lying open on top, next to a silver candelabrum. I gently

touch one of the candles and gasp: the wax is still warm! That means someone was in here recently!

I light the candles with my torch and lift the book to read the front cover: ***Vilificum Hex Colossum***. The title is written in gold text, and the front cover is decorated with some sort of purple stone, or perhaps a cloudy jewel. My heart beats faster as I realize I am holding incredible power in my hands.

I scan the contents pages: "Curses of the Ancients … The Cruelty Enchantments … Sinister Spells of the Silesians…"

The last one sends a chill down my spine: "The Darkness Hex". That sounds a lot like the curse Grandfather Oak mentioned in his story! My curiosity gets the better of me and I flip to the final chapter.

But it has been ripped out.

# CHAPTER 4

I slam the book shut, a cloud of dust erupting before me, blowing out the candles.

Someone, or something, has ripped out the whole chapter! A chapter that could contain a curse to ruin the world, to tip the balance of light and dark.

"Luna, let's get out of here!" I scoop up my little bundle of fluff and look up at the hole that we fell from. How do we get out?

Suddenly, the light from above disappears. Someone is there, watching us, blocking the hole. Thinking fast, I snuff out

my torch, plunging the cave into complete darkness. I quickly back up against the cold stone wall, holding my breath in terror.

Luna lets out a playful bark.

"Shhhh, Luna! Not now, it's not playtime!" I whisper.

The damage is done: whatever it is up there knows we are down here. I can hear it shifting its body at the entrance. Is it coming down? My body is shaking, so I hold Luna tighter and close my eyes....

**SPLAT!**

A freezing-cold snowball hits my forehead.

"Mittens!" I shout. Relief sweeps over me as I wipe the melting snow from my face. I relight my torch and see his pumpkin-shaped head shaking with laughter.

I have never been so pleased to see Mittens be so

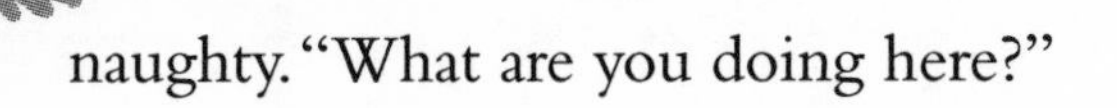

naughty. "What are you doing here?"

Luna leaps from my arms and skips around my legs, looking up at Mittens. He aims another snowball.

"Not now, Mittens! We need your help! Can you get us out of here?"

He brings his wooden finger to his chin. Apparently he needs to think this over!

"Mittens, c'mon! I need you!"

He tilts his head, considering.

I know what will work: "You will be my hero!"

Daylight pours into the cave as Mittens stands up tall and puffs his chest out, nodding triumphantly.

"Good job!" I look around and suddenly have an idea. "Luna, if we can drag that big bookcase

over here, and then climb up, we can throw Mittens the rope and he can pull us out!"

Luna barks in agreement as I begin to pull the heavy bookcase. It takes all my strength! Luna helps by pushing it with her front paws. After we get it in place, I grab the heavy rope, pull it over my shoulder and pick up Luna. I climb the bookcase until I am at very top. It wobbles beneath my weight.

"OK, Mittens, catch this!" I throw the rope up and he grabs it. Holding the other end tightly and with Luna secured in my other arm, I tell Mittens to pull.

Slowly, we begin to rise, my feet dangling over the cave. "Good boy, Mittens, keep going!" As we reach the mouth of the hole, I push Luna up before me and pull

myself out. On all fours, I am completely out of breath. And that is when I see Mittens.

My jaw drops. I begin to giggle. "Mittens! What are you wearing?"

Standing there looking very pleased with himself, Mittens is dressed up in my clothes! He's wearing my summer dress, emerald boots and a wide, floppy hat with brightly coloured flowers tucked into the band!

Mittens does a twirl and then looks up at the sun before looking back to me.

Suddenly I realize the reason for his crazy outfit. "Oh, of course! Snow golems can't

survive in the desert, so the clothes are protecting you from the sun!"

I stand up, brush the sand from my clothes and give him a hug. "Thank you for saving us, Mittens, you really are a hero! But you better go home now, or you'll melt!"

He looks to the ground.

"Please, Mittens? I need you to ... erm ... guard the house! Clearly you are a big, strong snow golem, so I need you to look after everyone, OK?"

Mittens suddenly raises a wooden finger, as if he's just remembered something. He digs around in the ruffles of his skirt (my skirt!), and pulls out a wooden bow.

"Katniss!" I cry out. "Oh, Mittens, you came to bring me my bow to make sure we would be safe. Thank you so much, you

lovely little thing. My hero!" I give Mittens's cheek a big kiss.

His orange face turns a distinctly redder hue, then he stands tall once again and nods before heading off towards home.

I smile to myself and watch his silhouette disappear over a mound of sand. He may drive me nuts, but I do love that boy.

"We better do something to mark up this hole so no animals fall down it, Luna." Rummaging in my backpack, I find some small wooden planks and some sticks. Using some string, I tie the small plank of wood to the wooden stick to create a sign. I find my big black permanent maker and write "DANGER" in big letters before using my hands to scoop up the sand into a little mound. I wonder how big I can make this mound? Oooooh, it could be a castle! I notice some small stones within reach and grab them. These could

be the pathway to the castle! And if we get some water, we could—

Luna snaps me out of my daydream with a playful bark.

I shake my head. "Oops! I do get carried away sometimes, don't I, Luna!"

Giggling, I plunge the sign into the top of the little sand mound and stand up. "There, that should be warning enough. Right, now where were we heading? Ah yeah, the forest! We need materials to build … erm, a thing!"

# CHAPTER 5

We can see the forest in the distance, at the other side of the meadow we're in. The long green grass and grasshoppers' chirps are a welcome change to the hot, shifting sands of the desert.

Luna playfully bites my boots.

"You're right, Luna, it's the perfect time for a picnic! I'm starving!" I unzip my backpack and lay out our food on a red-and-white checked picnic blanket. Apples, carrots and sandwiches for me, doggy food and doggy biscuits for Luna. She laps up the water I've poured into a bowl, splashing droplets

on her paws. I take a long drink from the bottle and feel the water instantly cooling my body down from the trek through the desert. There is a soft, peaceful breeze making the blades of grass dance, and the birds sing sweetly as they flitter above.

After our picnic, with my tummy perfectly full, I lay down and stare up at the clouds drifting slowly through the sky. I spot one that looks like an elephant riding a motorcycle.

"Ha, ha! Loves it!"

Another cloud looks like a giant mouse with a sword.

"Go find Captain Silverbeard, Mousie!" I urge him, giggling.

And there's one that looks like Mittens … doing something very rude! I frown and shake my head.

The storm clouds from this morning are still

hovering over the forest. "Hope it doesn't rain, Luna," I sigh. Rain always makes a mess of my hair.

Luna burps.

I sit up and begin to clear away our picnic and reload my backpack. "C'mon, then, cutie, let's get on with it before we get caught up in a storm."

Luna runs on ahead, investigating all the grasshoppers and playfully chasing the birds.

The edge of the West Forest looms ahead. This forest is one of my most favourites! The giant trees are almost like soldiers – tall, strong and mighty. Every time I come here, I always feel so small, like I am in some kind of fairy tale. I sometimes imagine the giant oak branches swatting away the night-time beasties like flies. Their giant roots acting like legs, they rip up the earth with each step they take, squishing the mean old beasties!

I come back to reality as the silence hits me. The birds

have stopped singing, and the grasshoppers have stopped chirping. Something doesn't quite feel right; the air feels different somehow. Goosebumps cover my arms.

"Luna?" I shout. I begin to feel wary as we get closer to the forest.

Luna bounds back to me, her ears flat against her head, her eyes wide. Something is really wrong.

"Stay behind me, Luna," I instruct as I pull Katniss from my bag. I creep past the giant trees that guard the forest edge.

We make our way deeper into the wood, but soon the sight before us stops us short and makes my blood run cold: the trees in the heart of the forest are dead! Every single one of them. The once glorious oaks are now just shells of what they used to be.

I slowly lower my bow. Tears fill my eyes as I look up at the decaying trees. There must be hundreds of them! Dead! How could this have happened?

I reach out my hand to stroke a rotting oak when Luna suddenly barks loudly and jumps up at me.

"What is it, Luna?" I ask, wiping at my eyes.

She points her snout to the bottom of the tree and growls. A translucent purple mist is crawling across the forest floor. Luna creeps towards the mist, but I gently pull her back as I bend down to examine it myself.

Fresh green shoots of new growth cover the forest floor, but as the mysterious mist swims over the tender leaves, they shrivel and turn brown.

"The mist," I whisper, horrified. I slowly walk backwards as it creeps towards us, clenching my fist around Katniss so tightly that my knuckles turn white. Purple, smoky tendrils reach only inches from Luna's paws, so I bend down and snatch

her up from the ground. It's then that I realize we are right under the angry purple clouds. Are the clouds and deadly fog connected in some way?

The mist forces us back out into the meadow, slowly eating everything in its path.

Could this be caused by the missing spell from that book? Unleashing darkness into the world? Whoever was down in that hole before me must have cast the Darkness Hex – and unleashed evil forces into the Land of Love.

Everything seems to move in slow motion. Before, the meadow had smelled of grass, sweet and herby, but now it smells of the tainted forest – death. And the mist is creeping ever closer.

I look behind me and see sparrows and blackbirds lining

the tree branches at the edge of the East Forest, on the other side of the meadow, their little heads tilted to one side. Their singing stops.

I see fear in their beady eyes.

I'm sure they see fear in mine too. This is no dream with crazy old pirates: this is my home under attack. I turn back and look at the dying forest. The mighty oaks that guard the forest edge wither, impossibly, before my eyes, their strong branches twisting and thinning out into blackened twigs. The whole forest now looks like a graveyard, with the trees frail and falling apart, like skeletons.

Suddenly everything is moving at normal speed again. I realize that I might not be the swashbuckling, brave hero of my dreams, but I have to at least try to save my kingdom. With a final glance at the forest, I hold Luna tight and head towards to the other side of the meadow towards the East Forest.

"We gotta find a way to stop this, Luna! We have the save the Land of Love!"

# CHAPTER 6

We reach the other side of the meadow, where the trees of the East Forest are healthy and strong – for now. I gently stroke the trunk closest to me, a birch tree. As I lay my hand flat along the Dalmatian-patterned bark, I feel a surge of warmth. The energy of the tree flows through me like electricity.

I look up to find every single bird watching me. Waiting for me. Counting on me.

The trees and animals are the very essence of the Land of Love. This is my kingdom, and I have to defend it. But where do I begin?

As if the birds can hear my thoughts, they begin to sing a sweet song. The music is mesmerizing, and I feel my arms relax, my shoulders droop. For a few moments the harmony infuses me and, smiling softly to myself, I forget the horrors of the mist.

But as the singing reaches its crescendo, the birds suddenly take off into the air, breaking me free from the trance. I watch as the blackbirds form a roiling cloud of wings, a spinning blur of feathers. There is a popping sound, and the birds suddenly scatter into the sky – all except the largest blackbird I have ever seen. He gracefully glides down and lands at my feet.

I've never seen birds do anything like that before, and I'm not sure what to think.

Luna fidgets and jumps from my arms. She circles the blackbird warily, sniffing at him with her nose.

I kneel down in front of him and look into his shining eyes, as yellow as the sun. His head tilts from side to side.

Luna stops circling him and sits next to him, her tail wagging. I take this as her stamp of approval.

"Mr Blackbird? My name is Amy. Do you know who did this?" I ask.

The blackbird nods.

"Can you help me? Can you take me to whoever did this?"

He nods again and suddenly takes flight, making me jump so much I fall backwards, narrowly missing some fox poop. As I stand up and brush the leaves from me, the blackbird hovers in the sky above me.

I have to decide: do I go home now and do what I can to defend my home and friends from this dark magic? Or do I follow this bird, and try to stop the spell at its source?

"Right, Luna!" I say, pretending to be confident. "We have to follow that bird and find out who's behind this!"

*I hope I've made the right decision*, I think to myself as I tread through the tall grass.

But I have to double back and pick up Luna. She spotted the fox poop and fancied a bath in it! Oh, why do dogs love fox poop so much? It's icky!

*   *   *

The sun is now at the edge of the horizon, pouring pink and amber light on the leaves of the trees and the large boulders scattered around us. I have never been to this part of the Land of Love before.

We have trekked far, passing from the meadow into a jungle, crossing plains, fording a number of rivers, and picking our way through rocky terrain. Despite a few hairy moments of having to pick Luna out of brambles after she gave chase to some rabbits, we have made good progress on a long, circuitous route that steered clear of the mist. I'm not sure I could even find my way back at this point.

But the blackbird seems to know which way to go, so Luna and I trudge forward.

We are climbing higher terrain now and can see the purple clouds over the West Forest slowly expanding, like some sort of bruise over the sky.

Climbing uphill, my boots are getting heavier with each step. The blackbird is perched on my left shoulder, his twig-like toes grasping me firmly. Luna is walking slowly, nearly stumbling, with her tail between her legs and occasionally bumping into rocks.

It's time for bed.

I light a torch from my backpack and examine our surroundings. Maybe we could make a tent from the picnic blanket, and I could stand guard all night with Katniss?

The beasties come out at night. I shudder at the thought of battling them. Or worse, failing at it.

No, we have to build some sort of protective structure, and quickly. Maybe if we use this rocky wall as a support, I could drag some tree limbs over—

Luna gives a whiney bark a little further up the mountain.

"Luna? What is it?"

As I reach her, the torch illuminates the mouth of a small cave. "Well done, Luna!" I pat her head and crawl into the cave, with the blackbird now having made himself some sort of nest in my hair. The cave is just big enough for us all, small and cosy. I grab some rocks and arrange them to hold my torch up in the middle of the floor.

A warm, orange glow fills the cave.

"This will do nicely," I mutter, as I head out again to gather some wood. It doesn't take long before I am able to cover the entrance up with branches and stones.

Just as I finish, I think I hear something moving around outside. I freeze, feeling my heart pound.

But I don't hear anything more. *Probably just my overactive imagination*, I tell myself. We will be safe here from beasties, at least for tonight.

I hope.

I sit down cross-legged. The blackbird flies from my hair and lands on my knee. Luna lazily nudges my backpack with her nose and looks up at me with those large puppy-dog eyes.

"You hungry, Luna? Let me

see what I have left from our picnic." I rummage through my backpack and find the rest of Luna's doggy food and treats, my bottle of water and a cookie. I pour some water into Luna's bowl and she gulps it straight down.

I pour a little water in the cap of the bottle and place it on the floor for the blackbird, along with half of the cookie. He dips his beak into the cap, then tips his head back to swallow the water. He pecks at the cookie, then looks me in the eye and nods his little head.

"You are very welcome!" I say as I bite into my half of

the cookie. I didn't realize how hungry I was! I soon finish it, savouring every single bite.

"Hmm," I say to myself. "If I had known that this was going to become a crazy adventure, I would have packed more food!"

I pull the picnic blanket from my backpack and wrap it around myself and Luna. The blackbird perches on my knee, his little legs soon swallowed by his body as he lowers himself down to get comfortable for the night. He sings a sweet lullaby, but even he is exhausted from the day. His song soon tapers off, his little eyelids close and he is asleep in seconds.

I'm not so lucky. Even though I am exhausted, I lie awake, staring at the rocky ceiling, watching a dangling spiderweb glisten in the torchlight. The sounds of the night – owls hooting, the wind

whistling and wolves howling at the moon – interrupt my troubled thoughts.

I can't stop thinking about that weird purple mist and the dead trees in the forest. Is Grandfather Oak's story true? Was he telling me about the Land of Love before I came here? Even if the story is true, why would someone want to bring dark magic back to the Land of Love?

Before I came here – hold on, why can I not remember anything before I arrived in the Land of Love? Every time I try to think back to my past, all I see is black. It's like I have no past … or I have blacked it out somehow. Where do I even come from?

I wish I could speak to Grandfather Oak now, having seen what I've seen today. I have so many questions.

I try to think back to whatever history I know about my land … but I come up blank. I'm ashamed to admit I know

nothing about the history of my land. Why can't I remember? Surely my parents—

WAIT. Do I even have parents? I realize, to my horror, that I can't even remember my parents!

I can only remember things up to a point, as if I had just dropped, fully formed and ready, into my own world. But that can't possibly be right. Can it?

I swallow hard.

I have to know. I have to fill in those blanks.

# CHAPTER 7

The dappled morning sun pierces through the cracks in the wooden branches and stones, and it burns through my eyes, forcing me awake.

For a split second, I forget where I am. I look around, wondering why I am lying on the ground in this tiny, closed-off cave with my dog and a random sleeping blackbird – when yesterday's events start to replay in my mind.

"Oh, right!" I say aloud, waking the little blackbird. "Sorry, little buddy, I didn't mean to startle you!"

Well, we're alive: my improvised wall did the trick!

The upsetting thoughts from last night start to bubble up in my mind, but I push them aside … for now. I need to get going, or I won't get answers to any of my questions.

I sit up and stretch out my arms. Strange: I don't remember dreaming last night. I almost miss Captain Silverbeard, even though he's always trying to get me with his sword…

"Wake up, Luna, we gotta save the world!" I give her a little tickle.

Luna rolls over and hides her sleepy eyes behind her silky ears. I give her another little tickle and soon she is up and ready to play.

As she and the blackbird chase each other around in the cave, I break down the wall and step outside and have another stretch, letting my eyes adjust to the bright sunshine.

All around me are mountains and tall pine and spruce trees. Snow caps some of the taller mountains in the distance. Our little cave appears to be part of a huge mountain that ascends into the sky, so tall I can't even see the top. I wonder if these are the mountains that I can see from my balcony, so far from here.

I feel a pang of sorrow, thinking of my friends back home. They must be so worried that Luna and I didn't come home last night. And I can't help but wonder what Mittens has been up to since I've been gone.

I look down towards the West Forest and the meadow, but I can barely see anything there through the violent purple haze. The clouds have doubled in size. The dark magic is spreading fast.

I gulp. We don't have much time.

The blackbird lands on my shoulder and gently pokes my cheek with his yellow beak.

"Do you still know where we are going?" I ask.

Another poke. I take that as a yes.

My tummy starts to rumble. "Oh, I wish we had some breakfast!"

The blackbird suddenly takes flight.

"C'mon, Luna. We gotta go!"

I grab my backpack and stow away the picnic blanket, torch and Luna's last biscuits. I break one in half and offer it to her.

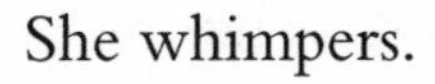

She whimpers.

"I'm sorry, Luna, but we have to ration out your food. I know it's not much, but I gotta make this last for you."

Gently she takes the biscuit half and frowns as she eats her breakfast. I'm sure she is trying to pout.

Soon we are ready to go. I scan the skies for our bird friend and find him a little way up the mountain by some bushes. As I climb towards him, he flies closer and places a blackberry at my feet.

"You found food!"

With a twinkle in his eyes, he nods his little head and hops towards the blackberry bushes.

They're loaded with berries! I carefully pick out the juiciest ones I can find, carefully avoiding the prickles. Then I rummage in my backpack and pull out the empty box that

contained my sandwiches from yesterday's picnic. It's a perfect storage container for the berries! I pass Luna the rest of her biscuit and gobble a few berries, the dark purple juice running down my wrist. "It's OK, Luna!" I say, my mouth full. "The blackbird found some food!"

Luna wags her tail as she munches up the rest of her biscuit and I pack away the berries.

"At least we won't go hungry now!"

The blackbird nods in agreement and takes flight, once more indicating the path. As he flies higher and higher, I realize he wants us to climb straight up the mountain.

Did I mention that this is the biggest mountain ***ever***?

"Oh, boy," I mumble. "I sure do hope he knows where he is leading us!"

Luna sets off in front of me, chasing butterflies up the mountain. As we start trudging, I try to imagine what I could build to make this climb easier. A massive escalator zig-zagging

up the slope? Hmm… I would need redstone for sure. Do I have enough redstone? Maybe I should go mining when I get home…

*If* I get home, that is.

# CHAPTER 8

"Are we nearly there yet?" I ask the blackbird. I am totally exhausted, and no matter how much we climb it seems we will never get to the top. Luna's little paws have given up, so I've tucked her in my backpack. I can feel her soft breath and wet nose on my neck as she naps.

Wouldn't it be nice if someone carried me around in a big backpack? It would have to be some sort of giant. Or maybe Bert is big and strong enough? Maybe I could invent something…

Each step up the jagged rocks feels like it takes all my

energy. My shoulders start to drop, and I am pretty sure at any moment I will be sleepwalking. Maybe I already am... Maybe this is just a dream! Maybe Captain Silverbeard is just around the corner, and he is—

**SPLAT!**

For a moment, my exhausted brain thinks I've been hit by one of Mitten's snowballs again. But it's not snow hitting my face; it's cold rain, forcing me back into reality.

"Arghh! My hair!" I panic as I try to cover my hair with my arms. Squinting at the sky with the rain falling on my face, it seems a storm is brewing. Now that we have entered the hazy atmosphere around the mountaintop, it's become dark. The clouds here have started to look a bit purple too, but I desperately hope it's just because of the storm.

OK, priorities: I need to save my hair or it will go all frizzy! I scan my surroundings and spot another cave mouth amongst the boulders. "C'mon, birdy!" I shout as the rain comes down harder. Thunder rumbles from the clouds above.

I sprint towards the cave and, once inside, sigh with relief. I gently lay down my backpack with Luna still napping inside, and carefully lift my torch out without waking her.

As the flames paint the inside of the cave with a soft glow, I notice markings on the rock wall.

I step closer, drops of rainwater falling from my hair and making dark spots on the dusty stone floor.

The wall markings look like … some sort of really old *drawings.*

The blackbird swoops in and lands on my shoulder. He shakes out his feathers, spraying me with a shower of water. "Thanks for that," I grumble as I try to wipe my face dry. "Hey, check this out."

I shine the torch closer to the wall, and I can make out a very faint stick man. Well, it looks like a woman, actually. She appears to be wearing a long dress and holding a stick. And it kinda looks like she is ... *laughing.*

The blackbird tilts his head as he examines the drawings too. The drumming sound of the rain outside is somewhat comforting; being here would be way scarier if it were deadly silent. I walk a little to the right, my torch lighting up other details of the drawings. There are some tangled bunches of lines

that look like spaghetti. The whole area is smeared with black smudges. But as I walk further on, the smudges disappear and there is just clean, bare rock with a few more drawn figures.

And there is another lady! This one is wearing a tiara. But it looks like she is running away from the first lady. "Oh! She looks like a princess!"

I turn to wake Luna to show her, but the blackbird pecks my cheek … hard.

"Ouch! What was that for?" I frown at him.

He looks to the drawing, and then to me. And then back to the drawing and to me again. And then he pecks me again.

"Hey, quit it! That hurts!" I say as I rub my cheek.

The blackbird rolls his little yellow eyes as he flies towards the drawing of the princess and pecks her cheek.

"Wait a minute..." I whisper.

*And then it hits me.*

"That's me?" I can't believe it! I wipe some of the dust away and look closer, my nose almost touching the cave walls.

I gasp. It *is* me! She's even holding my favourite flower!

My heart begins to race. "But what does this mean?" I feel my eyes go wide. I examine the first lady again. The spaghetti… No, wait. Those are spiders! And that's not a dress, it's a cloak! And that's not a stick, it's a wand!

**"ARRRGHH!! THE WITCH!"**

I scream, dropping the torch and sending the blackbird flapping away. Luna appears at my feet in attack position. The fur on her back is stiff, and she is growling, baring her teeth.

"No, Luna, it's OK, she isn't actually here... At least, I don't think so!" My hands start to shake as I bend down

and pick up the torch. The rain has stopped and now it is eerily quiet. The blackbird has landed in a corner, scared off by my scream. All I can hear is my own breathing and Luna's growling.

I stare at the whole wall, which I now clearly see is divided into two sections: a dark half and a light half. Grandfather Oak's voice replays in my mind: "Our world is a world of carefully calibrated balance..."

With my back against the cold, damp stone wall, I slide down towards the floor and hug my knees. How could I not see this before? *Of course* it's the Witch behind all this dark

magic; who else would it be? She has always wanted to ruin the Land of Love, ruin me. Ruin what I have created. I sniff loudly and blink hard, trying to keep the tears from falling.

Luna senses my fear and jumps up on to me, her paws dangling over my knees. She licks my chin. She doesn't look afraid; she looks brave. I know she would never let anyone hurt me, that she would risk her life to save me. But I don't want that. I am supposed to be ***her*** protector.

The blackbird lands on Luna's head, twitches his little wings and looks me in the eye. I smile weakly, putting on a brave face.

Suddenly, there's a clicking noise behind me, towards the back of the cave. I pick up my torch and direct it at the far end, where I notice a large hole in the back wall. Big enough for a person to squeeze through.

The clicking noise has grown louder and more intense. My heart beats fast. I can see something moving near the hole. Little black legs. Spiders! Hundreds of them!

I jump up, Luna falling from my knees, as hundreds – thousands! – of tiny spiders crawl through the hole and towards us. I point my flaming torch at them.

"STAY BACK!"

I yell. The flame dances, as my hands are shaking.

The spiders form a semicircle around us. Like a little army, they array themselves in a perfect pattern. They stand completely still now, watching us.

Luna growls at the spiders and gets ready to pounce. But it seems like the spiders are trying to tell me something; they suddenly reassemble and change formation, creating an arrow.

The arrow points towards the hole in the back of the cave.

"They want us to follow them," I whisper. I look down at Luna, who is still baring her teeth. The blackbird lands on

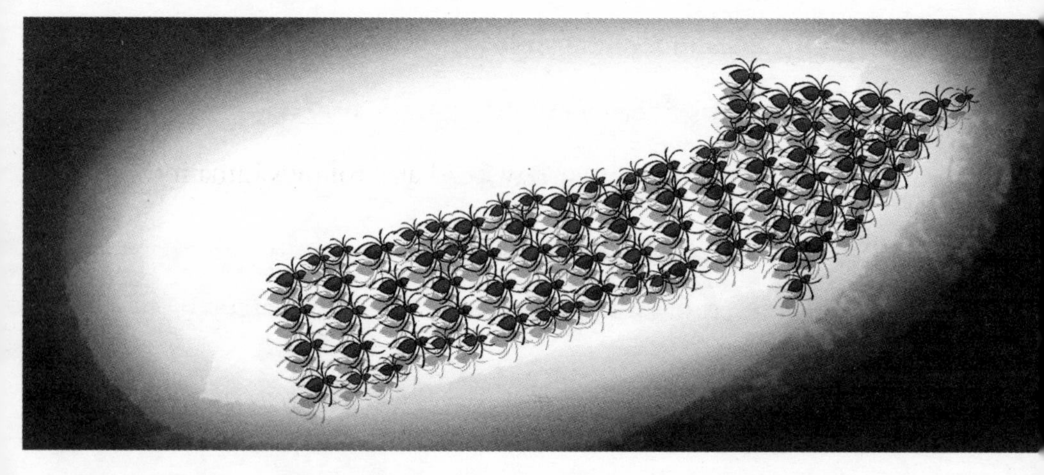

my shoulder and gently nibbles my ear. He points with his beak towards the spiders.

"I gotta follow them?" I ask meekly.

He nods his little head.

I sigh, my breath trembling. As I grab my backpack and tighten the straps, I grab Katniss and have her ready. "You guys stay here, OK? It could be really dangerous."

Luna gives me a dismissive look. Then she barks a loud, mighty bark and then leaps over the spiders and into the mouth of the cave. The darkness soon swallows her.

"Luna! Wait!" I shout. I should have known Luna would never let me go alone!

The blackbird flies over my head and follows Luna into the hole.

I'm suddenly aware that I am being watched by thousands of spiders' eyes. I bend down to address them. "I know who sent you. Take me to the Witch."

And with that, the spiders turn in unison and march into the hole.

I take a deep breath and follow.

# CHAPTER 9

Luna and the blackbird are waiting for me just beyond the hole, inside a bigger cave. My torch flame bounces around, making the hanging stalactites appear to wriggle. I can hear a faint dripping noise in the distance.

The spiders crawl past Luna, and the group of us march further into the mountain, with the blackbird flying between me and my dog. We seem to be moving up, towards the top of the mountain.

I pass a bunch of iron ore and coal and make a mental note to come back here to mine one day.

I shake my head: ***What am I thinking?*** I don't ever want to come back here!

Finally, I see a faint purple glow from up ahead, almost like a velvet blanket covering the jagged rock edges. I know we are close now.

I suddenly get goosebumps. ***Do dogs get goosebumps?*** I wonder as I look at Luna. ***Or would they be dogbumps?***
I shake my head again. ***No, Amy! This is not the time to get distracted!***

As we climb closer to the glow, I notice that it is a different type of purple from the mist that is destroying my world. This glow seems almost warm and inviting. The light is leaking from gaps in a large wooden door. The metal hinges and handle have been eaten by rust, and cobwebs have taken over the corners.

The spiders disappear, one by one, through the crack under the door. I can hear a bubbling noise coming from inside.

What do I do now? Do I knock? Do I just go in? Should I have Katniss drawn back, ready to fire?

I take a deep breath and decide that manners cost nothing in this world, but they could mean everything. I knock three big knocks, and the dust raised from the door makes me cough.

I hear a shuffling sound. Something is moving in there, but there's no answer.

I knock again.

More shuffling.

I can't wait any longer. I need to face this. The door handle is big, round and made of iron. As I grip the cold metal and turn clockwise, I can hear a lock being released. Slowly, I push open the heavy door, which swings wide with a deafening

CREEEEEEEAAAAAAAAK!

My heart is beating fast and I have to remind myself to breathe. As I enter the Witch's lair, I feel warmth from the purple glow, which seems to be flowing from a big silver cauldron in the middle of the cave room. Bookcases line the walls, as well as shelves packed with glass bottles of all sizes, all filled with brightly coloured potions. A fireplace in the corner makes the cave almost cosy, and in the other corner a massive book has been left propped open in a display case.

And it smells just like … a memory? I recognize the smell, but from where? As I try to remember, all I see is a blacked-out memory. Nothing.

As I slowly walk around, Luna trots along beside me, eagle-eyed. The blackbird has once again perched himself on my shoulder.

I pass some more shelves and glance at the items: jars of

dead bugs, silver and gold chalices, a stuffed raven, little gold pots, a skull with horns and a tank filled with tadpoles and newts. I'm surprised to see a window at the far side of the cave, and as I look outside I realize we are on the very top of the mountain. The clouds below cast a soft blanket, making my world invisible. The sky up here is deep purple.

Her world.

I suddenly remember the spiders. Where did they go? I look around, checking under the furniture and along the walls, but they have vanished.

I turn my attention to the book in the display case. I had thought it was lit from above, but now I realize that the

book itself is glowing! It must be enchanted! When I place my hand on the glass, I feel a charge in my palm. A strange poem is written on the page:

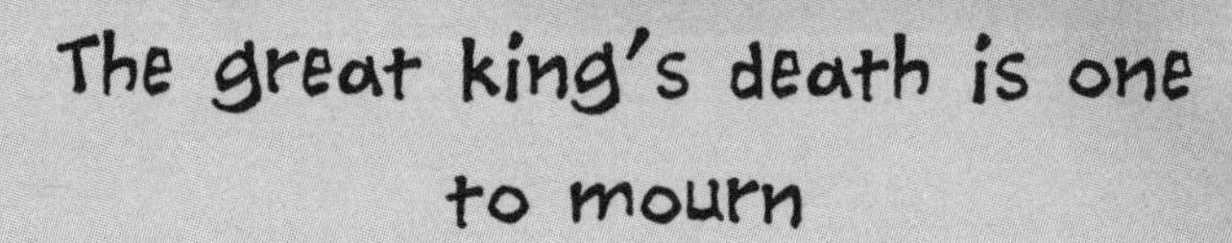

The great king's death is one
to mourn
In our land of peace and light.
A wretched darkness now is born
That no soul here is fit to fight.

Night will overwhelm its rival
Day will vanish from this world
Until an innocent's arrival
Love and peace will be unfurled.

Joy will blossom, darkness fading
All will toast the end to war
But shadows lie behind them waiting
Darkness stays for ever more.

Suddenly, I hear a loud creaking sound and, when I spin round, I find one of the bookcases has pulled away from the wall. A secret room!

I strengthen my hold on Katniss and slowly enter the passageway. It's a long tunnel – cold, damp and dark. I can hear the scuttling noise of thousands of spiders' legs.

**"EHEHEHEHEHEHEHEHE!"**

A piercing noise fills my ears. A witch's cackle – a laugh so evil it chills me to the bone.

My hands are now so sweaty that gripping Katniss has become difficult. A door appears out of the darkness. Before I am in touching distance, it swings open and standing before me is the Witch.

# CHAPTER 10

The Witch backs away from the door, as if welcoming me into the dark room. I have no idea what else to do, so I enter very cautiously.

I become aware of sinister forces everywhere, almost as if evil fills the air. This feeling is just like a sixth sense, and I wonder if I too am part of the magic here.

My eyes wide and my heart beating fast, I approach the Witch. Luna jumps in front of me, baring her teeth, but the Witch ignores her and keeps her gaze on me. Her pointed hat lies crooked on her knotted hair. Her long nose drips from her

face, complete with a large, hairy wart, and her piercing eyes are a vivid shade of purple.

"Hello there, child," she says, smiling with yellow crooked teeth. But nothing about her smile is kind.

Another feeling flows through my body. It's an emotion I am not used to: anger. I'm angry! I'm angry at the Witch! My eyebrows tighten as I look her in the eye.

"Why are you doing this?" I demand.

The Witch cackles again, chilling my angry blood. "My dear, I am merely doing what is right. You ruined my world, and I am merely putting it back to how it should be."

"Ruined? What do you mean?" I ask, my anger dimming further with confusion. I wonder whether the evil forces I feel

are messing with my emotions.

"My dear, the world was mine. Darkness reigned. Oh, how it reigned! Shadows thrived, and creatures out of nightmares roamed freely. But then you came along, and you tainted everything with your ... innocence." The Witch begins to pace the room. "Just like before when that awful prince took the world from me. But after years of searching through ancient libraries for the right spell, and years of planning, I took it back! And I'm no fool, I knew the prophecy: an innocent – you! – would destroy everything I had rebuilt. For years I waited, watching as the flowers returned in anticipation of your arrival. And then you came along, child, the perfect, oh-so-sweet little princess. So pure, so ... ***happy***. It was sickening. You even killed the last evil."

"The last evil?" I ask, confused. "I ... I don't understand!"

The Witch points her wand at me. "My dear friend Thorne! A magnificent tree who just oozed darkness. He

possessed powers greater than your imagination. But he grew weaker once you showed up. He knew what was going to happen, and he warned me. It was you, dear, who was to kill him. And you did. You killed Thorne!"

My heart beating fast, I still fail to understand.

"You didn't even know, did you?" the Witch spat. "To you he just looked like a normal tree. You needed wood, so you killed him." She stopped pacing and turned to me with a wicked smile. "But, child, all is not what it seems. From Thorne dropped a sapling. Which you, being the cute little flower child you are, replanted. The roots of evil grow in that tree, dear one, the tree you call Grandfather Oak!"

I take a step back in shock, my back now against the cold stone wall. "No! You're lying!" I shout. "Grandfather Oak is not evil!"

"Isn't he?" she snarls. "Well, the prophecy's not over yet, girl. You may have brought joy to this land, but the shadows are done waiting. ***Darkness stays for ever more!***"

The Witch sees my expression and chuckles – an ugly, throbbing sound. "Dear, you look so surprised. Well, I suppose that makes sense. You don't know this world's past. You don't even know where you come from, do you? Still have black spots in your memories?"

The Witch cackles again, and it feels like my heart has stopped. How does she know that I have gaps in my memories?

"I am the rightful queen of this land," she snarls, "not

you, Princess. Don't you get it yet? It's been foretold!"

Wait a minute… Queen? Does that mean that the Witch was once a … princess? Is that possible? But if I'm a princess now, does that make her the queen? Does that make her my—

"Oh, no, child, it's not like that," she says, reading my expression and grinning at me. "I'm not your mother. Not quite."

Not quite?! What does that mean? ***Wake up, Amy, wake up!*** This has to be a horrible dream…

"And now it's time for me to take my world back," the Witch continues. "And then some. With the death of Thorne, I took action. Ancient dark magic led me to the book I have been searching for, hidden under the desert. With that book I was able to create a new Darkness Hex, and now it's more powerful than ever! Say goodbye to your precious Land of Love!"

The Witch's words hit me like ice-cold water. I shout,

"I'm sorry I took the world from you – I think – but you can't take it back," I plead. "The Land of Love is a home – a home to many innocent animals and creatures. It's a safe place!"

"Not any more." She points her wand at me, and, before I can react, a magical web shoots from the end of it and pins me against the wall. The web crawls up my body as if alive and wraps itself around my wrists and ankles.

Luna leaps in the air, her teeth bared, but the Witch is too fast.

**ZAP!**

Luna is trapped in a cage made of more magical spiderwebs.

I struggle to get free, but the web around my wrists pulls tightly like rope, holding me in place. "Let me go!" I demand, straining against the webs. But they seem to get tighter the more I wriggle.

The Witch laughs at my feeble attempts to get free. "Hush now, child." With another wave of her wand, another web shoots out and plasters itself on my mouth, pulling my lips together like glue.

Luna barks aggressively, and the Witch shoots another web at her, gagging her. Luna whimpers, and my heart aches that I am unable to protect her.

"Now the final part of my plan. Spiders, come to me," she demands.

The army of little spiders re-emerges from the darkness and assembles in front of where I hang from the wall. Their beady eyes watch me as I try to shake loose, but it's impossible.

The Witch's own eyes are shining. "It's time," she whispers.

Suddenly the spiders start moving, crawling all over each other until they create a shape taller than the Witch herself. I stare in disbelief, panic running through my veins, as the shape grows and grows. The mass soon has legs, eight of them, until the thousands of spiders have created one giant spider – a spider so big its back touches the ceiling of the cave room.

I try to scream, but the sound barely escapes the

web covering my mouth. I shake my head from side to side, trying desperately to get free as the giant spider slowly steps towards me.

"My babies haven't eaten in a very long time," the Witch says. "I have promised them a feast they will never forget. Goodbye, Princess!" And with a mighty swoop of her deep purple robes, she leaves.

The mass of spiders advances towards me. It raises a giant spider leg to stroke my hair, which sends about a million shivers down my spine. Tears sting my eyes as I frantically look around the cave for something – anything – to help me.

Luna, whimpering through her gag, paws desperately though the bars of her spiderweb cage.

There is no way out. The web that restrains me is too strong. Each time I struggle, the web gets tighter, until my wrists feel like they are on fire.

The giant spider pincer mouth opens, revealing a dark hole and making me recoil. I am going to be spider food. There is no one to save me now: no Mittens, no Bert and no Bertha.

I can't even save myself.

# CHAPTER 11

As the giant spider inches closer, I struggle to remain calm. My muffled screams for help are just as useless as Luna's desperate whimpers.

All of a sudden, I hear the flapping of small wings.

The blackbird! He swoops in through the cave window and hovers between me and the eight-legged beast, his wings creating a soft breeze on my face.

And then I hear the sweetest music I have ever heard. The blackbird has begun to sing. The song is mesmerizing, and I can't help but relax as my body goes limp.

The giant spider twitches, several thousand eyes blinking at the blackbird. Luna has stopped barking, the only noise being the sweet song and the scuttling of the spiders struggling to keep form.

As I watch the blackbird gracefully fly around our heads, my eyes feel heavy and my head falls forward.

I shake my head. ***This is no time to sleep, Amy!*** I tell myself. I yawn and blink slowly ... and then blink again ... and then ... and then...

Captain Silverbeard falls into the ocean with a mighty splash.

"Ha-ha! You're toast, old man!" I shout, waving my pink jewelled sword as I peer down from the edge of the ship.

"Never! You aren't strong enough, little girl! I will take

back the town of Driftwood, and it will be mine! You will never beat me, Princess!" He bobs around like a cork, his silver beard floating before him.

"Oh yeah?" I taunt. "But I've already beaten you!" I raise my chin to the blazing sun.

Captain Silverbeard swims towards me. "Well, what about the spiders?" he asks, smiling. His gold teeth flash in the sun.

I'm confused. "What do you mean, 'spiders'?" I ask.

Suddenly, I feel something tugging at my boot. I look down, but there is nothing there. I can hear a soft whimper.

"Wait! What's going on?"

I stumble backwards until I feel my back up against a wall. The sun has dissolved into the ocean, and the ocean has dissolved into the ship. All I can hear is Captain Silverbeard laugh his husky laugh, and I can feel something still tugging at my boot. My eyes close.

"Where did you go?" I mumble as my eyes open.

As the room adjusts and my head stops spinning, I realize I am in a cave. Luna is at my feet, biting through what

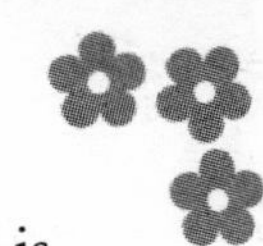

appears to be spiderwebs pinning me to the wall. A blackbird is pulling the web from my wrists.

It was a dream! I must have fallen asleep.

Panic strikes as I remember what happened. The giant spider! It must have collapsed on the floor, where there are now hundreds of sleeping spiders in a mound, as if someone had swept them up with a broom. The blackbird must have freed Luna from her web cage, and now they are freeing me.

After the blackbird loosens the webs on my wrists, I am able to free them and pull apart the webs restraining my arms. I pull away the web covering my mouth and breathe deeply. I then rub my wrists, which are covered in sore red marks.

"How did you do that?" I ask the blackbird.

He twitches his head, his little beady eyes bright.

I pull my body from the wall and use all my strength to escape the last of the webbing, falling forward to my knees.

Luna jumps around me, licking my face. I draw her to me and cuddle her. "I'm so sorry, Luna," I say.

The blackbird lands on my shoulder and gently nudges my cheek with his little head.

I gently stoke his chest with my finger. "Thank you so much," I whisper. "The Witch is on her way to take over the rest of the Land of Love. We have to get back and protect the others."

I stand on wobbly legs and take a deep breath. It's time to be brave. My family need me.

"Come on, guys, we have to go home."

# CHAPTER 12

The Witch has left the lair, I can feel it.

As we make our way out the dark, damp tunnel, past the flowing cauldron and through the warm purple glow, I try to figure out how I can to defeat the Witch. I don't like to fight. Nothing is resolved with fighting. But what other choice do I have? The Witch is relentless; she will stop at nothing.

And if it's all fated to happen, according to the prophecy, is there any point in fighting it?

Luna bounds ahead of me, sniffing every rock we pass, and

the little blackbird flies on ahead, swooping this way and that.

I smile to myself a little. This tiny blackbird saved me from the jaws of thousands of tiny spiders. A little stranger, yet he risked his life for me.

The cave gets brighter the further we go. The shadows crawl higher, creating jagged patterns on the cave walls. I think about the idea that light cannot exist without darkness. And vice versa. Just like Grandfather Oak said, "***One cannot exist without the other.***"

My heart hurts as I think about Grandfather Oak. He can't come from Thorne! Grandfather Oak is a kind, wonderful spirit! But why would the Witch lie about that?

We walk on, each of us left to our own thoughts, and it feels like ages before we reach the smaller cave with the old drawings.

Basking in the morning sun, the drawings are barely visible

in the brightness. I stop for a moment and stare at them, the little stick princess and the little stick witch. A prophecy. My destiny.

I gently trace my finger along the little me, the funny wavy lines of my hair. I can change my destiny ... right?

I straighten up and tighten the straps of my backpack. "C'mon," I say and step outside, into the fresh mountain air. I may not know anything about my past – or about my future – but I do know my friends. And prophecy or not, right now they need me.

The brightness of the sun is blinding, so I cover my eyes

with my hands, peering through the gaps of my fingers until my vision adjusts. It is still eerily quiet up here. No birds sing, no grasshoppers chirp and the sky is still purple above the clouds. The ground has dried, all dusty and chalky, creating little puffs of powdered earth wherever my boots hit the ground.

I walk fast, almost stumbling down the mountain, eager to get home and protect my family.

The meadow is dead. The mist has eaten the grass, devoured it, leaving behind singed blades and powdered ash. A sinister purple haze hangs over it all.

When we had descended down the mountain, I couldn't believe my eyes. The purple storm cloud had grown double in size yet again, and it was still on the move. It had passed through the meadow and left a wasteland behind.

"Where is she?" I whisper as Luna whimpers at the

sight before us.

The West Forest, the meadow … the desert!

"I have an idea," I say, and I begin to run along the edge of the blackened meadow, carefully keeping clear of the purple mist. The blackbird flies ahead, and Luna sprints alongside me.

Finally, I reach the hole in the desert with my "DANGER" signpost. Thankfully, the mist hasn't come through here. The rope is still lying here, off to the side. I quickly tie one end to a nearby boulder.

"Luna, keep watch. I'll send the blackbird up to you if I'm in trouble down there. And keep an eye on that mist! Bark if it gets too close!"

Luna begins to circle the hole, on patrol. The blackbird

lands on my shoulder, and together we make our way down the rope, one hand moving to grip the rope after the other.

At the bottom, I light the torch. Everything looks just as I left it.

I run over to the bookshelf. *Magic for Beginners, White Magic, Powerful Magic*. I pull *Powerful Magic* from the shelf and bring it over to the desk, where I light the candelabrum. The blackbird hops on to the desk, carefully avoiding the dripping wax.

"Come on, come on," I mumble, flipping through its pages.

"Aha!" I shout as I find what I am looking for. "'Powerful Counter Spell'," I read. "This might just work!"

The blackbird hops on to the page, his little head

moving from left to right as he reads. He looks up to me and shakes his head sadly.

"No? Let me try anyway." I clear my throat and straighten up as I read aloud the incantation. It's in a funny old language, but I sound out the words as best I can. It's only a half a dozen or so lines long, so it doesn't take long to finish:

"Parconem ralaki pilter hogola
Algana pippernid floxo
Calabinaki orgelum quandi epalin
Siport clintoker frylo gromenid poid
Delolon fiffin renoxida wix
Ponidzum fulimaqua eb gortopy!"

I look around expecting something. I don't really know what, but … something.

A minute passes.

Nothing.

"OK, how about… 'Powerful Lightness Spell'? That should fight off darkness, right?"

Again, the blackbird shakes his head.

I frown, but I read out the words anyway:

**"Vordna renoxis balaclan, firn legowitz slonaka blan…"**

I try to go slow, but it's hard not to trip over the words.

**"…orn cornilia luminous palaxis!"**

I suddenly feel a wind in my hair, goosebumps invade my skin, and the room around me glows brighter

and brighter…

"It's working!" I cry. "We did it!" I feel my spirits rise…

But wait: it's not my spirits rising, it's me! I'm floating!

Suddenly the glow flickers like a bulb, and I drop back down to the ground with a thump.

"No!" I cry and bury my face in my hands. As the light disappears, so does my hope.

"I guess that wasn't about light, it was about being light." I close the book with such force, the candles go out. "And it didn't even last long. None of these spells are going to work, are they?"

The blackbird shakes his head once more.

Luna barks from above.

"Come on, Mr Blackbird, let's get going. It was worth a try, but time is running out. Let's get back to the house."

After I climb out of the cave, I see that the mist has reached the edge of the desert. I swallow hard and start making our way towards home.

I can see the roof of my home on the horizon, but the purple mist is scarily close. Huge storm clouds fill the sky, blotting out the sun. But where is the Witch?

I can't waste another second.

When I reach the entrance, I see that Bert and Bertha have come to greet me, and I suddenly find myself diving into their arms.

"Oh, Bert! Bertha! We are in big trouble!" I mumble through tears. I barely come up to their chests, my ear resting on Bert's cold stomach as they hug me in a joint embrace.

We go inside and I hear the sound of paws making their way downstairs, and I turn just before I am overwhelmed by a stampede of dogs, their wagging tails slapping me in the face. I laugh through my tears as I fall to the floor.

Lexi, Max, Mars, Sailor, Lola, Romeo, Boomer and Destiny jump all over me, covering me

in a blanket of doggy fur and kisses.

"I missed you guys too!" I laugh.

Then I am headbutted by my three cats, all purring and softly meowing. I tickle their chins before standing up and brushing all the fur to the ground.

The blackbird lands on one of Bert's shoulders, and I realize my cats look very interested in him, their tails curling like snakes.

"No no no, kitties, this blackbird is family now, OK?"

With just those words, their hunting eyes soften and they sit, having suddenly lost interest in him.

"We need to have a family meeting" My voice starts to shake a little as I realize time is moving fast. "Max, can you collect

the snow golems and bring them to the Meeting Room?"

Max barks and, with his tail wagging, runs upstairs.

"OK, let's go, gang." I have to take deep breaths and compose myself. I have to be a good leader, I have to be calm. If I panic, they will all panic.

I enter the room and stand by the window as everyone files in and takes their seats. I look out the window over the Land of Love. I can see Peace Pig and Peace Chicken bathing in the Peace Pool. I can see the stables, the Gingerbread Teahouse, and the show-jumping course where I compete with my horses. I see the great lake, filled with friendly squids. My Land of Love.

And I can see a huge purple storm cloud approaching fast, above a rolling purple mist.

**SPLAT!**

A freezing cold snowball splatters on the back of my head, making me jump.

"Mittens!" I shout. I turn around to find Max leading my three snow golems into the room, and Mittens's eyes are wide and full of mischief as usual. "Everyone sit, OK? We need to talk about something very important."

Mittens's eyes fall, a look of concern spreading across his pumpkin face. As he and the other snow golems take their seats, the room is filled with the sound of purring cats, whimpering and panting dogs and the creaking of iron golems.

"Something serious has happened. We are all in very grave danger."

# CHAPTER 13

I tell them everything. I can't protect them by shielding them from the truth.

Er, except the part about the prophecy, that is. Looking into their concerned eyes, I can't bear to tell them that darkness is fated win in the end.

When I finish, Max, Mars, Sailor and Lola all jump on to the desk, barking loudly. Bert and Bertha stand up so suddenly, their eyebrows furrowed, that their chairs fall to the floor. The others gather at my feet, staring up at me with bright, worried eyes.

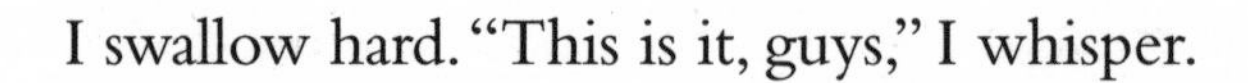

I swallow hard. "This is it, guys," I whisper.

I look to Mittens – my clown, my little comedian – and see a frozen icicle below his eye.

"I don't know where the Witch is now, but she's coming. And I don't know if there's a way to stop her, but I'm going to try." I smile with as much confidence as I can muster. I have to show them I'm not afraid. I have to … ***believe*** I can do this. And I have to make that belief happen.

I pull Katniss from my backpack and make my way out of the Meeting Room, feeling my family's eyes on me.

Seconds later, the loud clattering sound from behind me causes my heart to swell; they would never let me fight alone. I reach out a trembling hand to open the front door.

The sight before me takes my breath away. On the horizon, just beyond the Enchanted Treehouse, the purple mist is rising high like a tidal wave, killing everything it touches. A storm paints the sky a violent purple, with booming thunder and flashes of lightning. The Witch herself is front and centre, leading the mist and a huge army of spiders. But she's also brought monsters with her: terrifying skeletons and zombies with bits of flesh falling from their faces.

"That's where she's been!" I say to myself. "Gathering all the beasties who come out at night."

Darkness's revenge on the light.

I feel a light pressure on my shoulder; the blackbird has perched there once more.

Trembling, I make my way across the bridge, the dogs behind me alert, their tails pointed high like arrows, their heads low and their eyes sharp.

Great trees fall in the distance as the mist takes them down one by one, like a mudslide crashing down a mountain. Each step I take seems to last for ever, and it saps my energy.

I look down to the lake below and see the squid and fish swimming merrily, blissfully unaware of the approaching danger.

But I am petrified. I can feel each beat of my heart through my entire body.

As I reach the end of the bridge, I turn to my dogs. "If this goes bad, I want you guys to run, OK?" Mars tilts his head as the other dogs let out soft whimpers. "I mean it. Promise me. I want you to run as fast and as far as you can."

Sailor licks my hand as I turn to face my doom.

The Witch halts about a dozen yards away, and as she does the spiders, beasties and mist come to a complete stop behind her.

"You may have escaped my trap, child," she snarls, "but there is no escape now."

Mars, Max, Sailor and Lexi leap in front of me, teeth

bared and growling at the enemy. I breathe deeply, and tighten my grasp on Katniss.

"You say that you and your beasties thrive in darkness," I say. "But don't you understand that darkness cannot exist without light?"

She moves closer, the spiders and mist following her.

"We can work together," I offer.

The Witch cackles. "Ha! Together? No, child, I don't need anything from you. I'm taking the world so my creatures can thrive, so I can rule. You walk around with your little animals, with your flowers, and think you can bargain with me?" Her angry eyes bore through me.

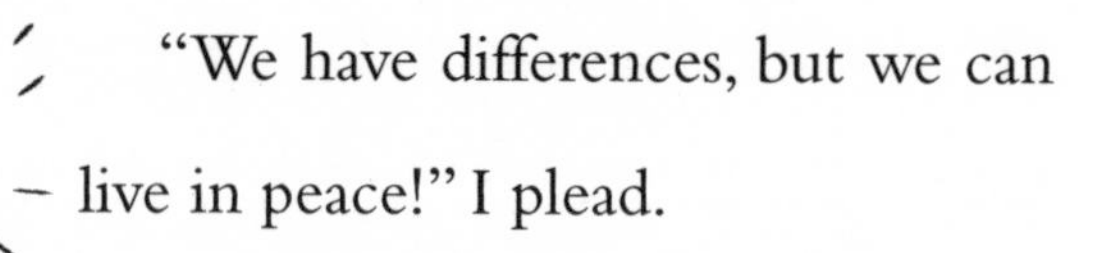

"We have differences, but we can live in peace!" I plead.

"Never!" she screams, raising her wand and shooting a magical web.

I duck, throwing the blackbird

into flight, and the web narrowly misses me – but it hits Lexi, the eldest of my dogs, instead.

"Lexi!" I shout. She is pinned to the ground in the sticky web, so I fall to my knees, frantically trying to rip it away.

Mars and Max run towards the Witch, growling loud.

"No! Come back!" I cry.

I watch helplessly as my faithful dogs charge. Mars reaches the Witch first and jumps for her wand, but she flings him overhead and into the mist. I watch in horror as Max runs after him, the mist swallowing them both. Sailor, Lola and Romeo have also charged ahead of me, and they begin to fight the spiders and beasties. Mr Frost, Blizzard and Mittens glide past, throwing snowball after snowball at the Witch. But the frozen missiles seem to bounce back before making contact, almost as if there is a force field protecting her.

Suddenly, I hear a sound that chills my blood – a piercing howl, a demonic howl.

A bloodthirsty howl.

I watch in horror as Max and Mars emerge from the mist and stand either side of the Witch. Their eyes glow red, their fur is raised in jagged spikes, and their jaws hang open, dripping drool on to the ground. The Witch smiles and pets their heads. Romeo backs away from the spiders and edges towards Mars, sniffing, but Mars lunges, snapping his jaws at him.

I scream.

Strength from deep within me helps me pull the web apart and free Lexi. I get up unsteadily while Lexi steps over to join Luna, Boomer and Destiny, who are watching the battle in shock.

The snow golems have lowered their snowballs as it has sunken in that Mars and Max are … *changed*. Romeo just manages to escape and runs back to me, whimpering.

"Sailor! Lola! Come back now!" I scream.

They sprint back to me, their eyes alive with terror. The Witch cackles as lightning strikes behind her, illuminating her silhouette.

Max and Mars stare at me hungrily, creeping closer. I slowly walk backwards and raise Katniss. I have to defend my family.

My hands shaking, I pull the string back and take aim at the Witch. I release the arrow, and it flies through the air.

But before it can reach its target, it bounces back. There is a force field protecting her!

It's hopeless. I lower my bow as I continue to walk

backwards, my feet finding the oak wood of the bridge. The Witch advances, the beasties following in awkward lunges and the spiders crawling behind her with their giant legs creeping hypnotically.

Mars stalks ahead of Max and stand yards in front of me, his lips curled back and jaws snapping at the air.

"Mars, honey? It's me," I call out in a shaky voice. He suddenly runs towards me at full speed.

Does he remember me? Has the Witch's spell been broken?

He leaps, pushing me to the ground with a thud. He

stands on my chest and snaps his teeth in my face! I manage to grab hold of his collar, pulling him away to stop him biting me. "Mars, it's me!" I plead. "It's Amy!"

I look into his red eyes, but I cannot see Mars. I see a stranger. Mars is gone.

The other dogs tackle Mars to the ground, but he squirms away and retreats to the Witch's side.

I stand, my legs shaking, and wipe Mars's drool from my clothes. I turn to the dogs and snow golems. "I'm sorry," I whisper.

Mittens comes forward and wipes a tear from my eye with his little stick finger. He turns to Mr Frost and Blizzard, and they nod at him, and they all suddenly launch snowballs over my head – hundreds of them!

They fly straight towards the enemy, but bounce back from the force field.

I am proud of their determination, but I know we are doomed.

"Guys, remember what I said? Run! Save yourselves! Please!"

But they don't. They just look at me, with love and courage in their eyes. I turn back and retreat over the bridge, and they follow me.

Meanwhile, the Witch has moved on to the Enchanted Treehouse. I watch in horror as my creation is eaten by the mist. It falls with an almighty crash to the ground and dissolves.

She reaches the bridge as I lead my group further back. I remember the fishes and the squid down in the lake, and I have to close my eyes as the mist glides over the water, turning it black.

It's hopeless.

At the entrance of my house, Bert and Bertha stand guard like soldiers, ready to defend our home. Saturn, Comet and Star stand at their feet, their claws out and ready to fight, hissing at the purple storm.

I don't know what to do. What can I do?

I look at my dogs, my cats, my golems and the blackbird. Each of them is prepared to fight. But what would be the point? We are never going to win against this dark magic.

The Land of Love is over. She has won.

# CHAPTER 14

Grandfather Oak! I suddenly remember the story he told this morning.

Instead of retreating into the house, I run towards him as fast as I can.

"Grandfather!" I sob as I hold him tightly. I feel the roughness of his trunk against my skin, and my tears run rivulets along his bark.

"Amy, dear. Look at the flowers."

I open my eyes and glance at the red lovely-bubbly love-love petals that I planted around Grandfather Oak.

They are dead. The once ruby-red petals are now just crispy brown shells.

"But why are they dead?" I ask through my tears. "The mist hasn't reached them!"

Grandfather Oak smiles, moving the wrinkles of the bark.

"You are the very essence of this world! You have a connection with all that is happy and peaceful. The flowers know this. When you give up hope, they give up hope too. The Land of Love is dying because your hope is dying."

I sniff back more tears. "But how can I fight the darkness?"

"Darkness and evil cannot be overcome. Two forces as strong as light and darkness will never overpower each other. What changes the world is what is in your heart."

I swallow hard as I remember the Witch's story of Grandfather Oak's origin. I let go of the tree and take a small step back.

"Grandfather? Th-the Witch told me about … Thorne," I sputter.

Grandfather Oak smiles warmly.

"Did you ever wonder why the spell started in the West Forest, and not from the Witch's lair? The spell started where he grew. My father, Thorne."

I gasp. "It's true? But … he was bad!"

"Yes, he was," Grandfather Oak agrees.

"But you're not bad," I say, confused.

He laughs. "No, dear, I am not bad. My heart is pure, and darkness does not run through my branches. I may have sprouted from Thorn's tainted seeds, but you found me, a sapling, and planted me here, Amy. With all the love and nurturing you gave me, I am who I am today. As I told you before, good can come from bad."

I step closer to Grandfather Oak and

place my palm on his bark, feeling his warm energy. "But, Grandfather, what do I do now? I saw the prophecy in the Witch's lair, and it says that darkness stays for ever more. I can't fight, I can't win!"

Panicking, I realize the storm clouds are directly overhead, which means the Witch is close by.

A loud cracking noise makes me jump. The entrance doors to my house have splintered as the mist invades the building. She must be inside the house, looking for us. The mist is rolling on around either side of the building, heading our way.

"Battles aren't always won by fighting," Grandfather Oak replies. "And don't forget what I told you this morning. Hope is a very powerful force. Use the pureness of your heart,

for love will always win in a war against hate."

With my heart beating fast, I hug Grandfather Oak as tightly as I can. I look at Bert and Bertha, my big iron soldiers, and stretch my hand out to them. They wrap their arms around Grandfather Oak, and the dogs then follow suit, wrapping themselves around my legs and the tree. Mittens, Mr Frost and Blizzard wrap themselves behind me, holding hands with themselves and Bert and Bertha. The cats climb up the bark and cling to a strong branch.

I look to my right and find Peace Chicken perched on Peace Pig's back. The two of them are leading my four horses, Journey, Lilly, Tinkerbell and Moonbeam, and my donkey, Gabriel. They gently nudge me with their soft, velvety noses before leaning their heads against the old tree. My family.

The mist is now yards away. My hair flies about in the storm's wind, and Grandfather Oak's leaves rustle loudly.

I can barely breathe as fear spreads through my body, making it numb. The cats climb down Grandfather Oak and snuggle with the dogs, each animal resting their head against the bark. The blackbird flies from Bert's shoulder on to my own and gently head-butts my damp cheek.

"There you are!" I hear the Witch say. She's found us. "Urgh, what a pathetic sight!"

The mist is now just yards away, and the Witch and spiders are getting closer and closer.

"What? Are you not going to fight me, little tree-hugger?" she snarls.

The mist… Here it comes.

I breathe heavily and turn to my family. "I love you guys, more than you will ever know," I say quickly. "Thank you for your kindness and your love. I am so grateful to have the best family I could ever have wished for!" I can barely get the words out, my voice is so shaky.

"I love you, Grandfather Oak. I love you, Luna. I love you, Mittens..." I go on telling each of my family members that I love them. It's almost like a prayer, or an incantation. A sparkle shimmers through me as I list the names.

"...I love you, Mr Frost. I love you, Comet..."

The sparkle grows within me, blossoming, from my toes to the top of my head. With each name, I feel more at peace and I suddenly find myself smiling.

"...I love you, Blizzard. I love you, Journey."

I've run out of names. But then I think about my bravest dogs of all, Mars and Max, who sacrificed themselves to

save me. I look back over my shoulder to see them advancing towards me with their new master, the Witch.

"I love you, Mars. And I love you, Max." I start to feel dizzy, my head feeling warm. And even though all is lost, I look up and smile at the love all around me.

"Love will always win," Grandfather Oak whispers.

I hug him tighter as the mist reaches my boots. I close my eyes.

# CHAPTER 15

A forceful wind washes over us. I hold Grandfather Oak tightly and use my legs to pin my animals as close to him as possible. I scream, and struggle to remain focused. I hold on for dear life, my eyes clenched closed and my ears filled with the sound of thunder and rushing wind.

And then, suddenly, it stops.

With the hurricane wind gone, I fall to the ground, completely disorientated. Lying on my back, I try to open my eyes, but the brightness hurts them, and I use my hands to shield them from the light. I peer through my fingers.

It's … the sun!

As my eyes slowly adjust, I sit up, dazed and confused. My dogs are lying on the ground panting. Bert and Bertha are helping each other up. Mittens's head has fallen off, and Mr Frost and Blizzard are trying to put it back on. Star, Saturn and Comet are brushing their coats, not impressed with the dust that has covered them.

I look behind me. My house is no longer in ruins. The bridge, the enchanted treehouse – everything is how it was, and how it should be. I turn back to Grandfather Oak.

"Wh-what happened?" I ask, rubbing my head.

"Your light destroyed the darkness, dear," he answers.

"But how?"

"The battle of light and dark shifted once again, so the power of white magic became stronger than dark magic."

"White magic? But we didn't cast any spell! I don't understand!"

"Dear, you *did* cast a spell; you just didn't know it! Magic is really just emotions that gain enormous power, and your love spell, in which you told us all how you loved us, conquered the darkness. Even in complete darkness, your light shone through, extinguishing the dark."

I brush the dust from my body as I stand, wobbling a little. I help Lexi and Destiny up, as they seem to be struggling a bit, too.

"It's... It's over?" I ask, confused.

"Yes, my dear, it's over. The Witch and her creatures have gone. The spell has been broken."

"Gone? As in for ever?"

"I'm not sure about for ever," he says, smiling. "As you know, light cannot exist without some darkness."

"But what about the prophecy?"

Grandfather Oak frowns. "Darkness stays for ever more. I wonder if the Witch misunderstood the prophecy, thinking

it meant she would take over the Land of Love? It must mean something else entirely…"

The thought finally starts to sink in: *We are safe!* The Land of Love is safe again!

I jump in glee as my dogs run around my legs, jumping up playfully. Then I drop to my knees, opening my arms as they pile on for cuddles. I stroke their heads and ruffle their ears.

And then I remember, and suddenly lose my smile. I

bow my head as tears sting my eyes. "Mars and Max," I whisper.

The other dogs sit and stare at each other, their ears hanging around their faces, their noses to the ground. And they begin to cry.

"I'm so sorry," I whisper through tears.

The howls and whimpers tear through my heart. Bertha wraps her cold iron arm around me as I turn and cry on her shoulder.

Suddenly, I hear faint barking in the distance.

Woof! Woof! Woof! Woof! Woof! Woof!

I look over Bertha's shoulder, and my heart almost stops. There are Mars and Max, bounding around the corner of my house, their tongues flapping in the wind!

It can't be! I literally crawl over Bertha's shoulder and fall to the ground as Max and Mars leap in the air. I catch them and fall to my back as they lick away my tears, their tails slapping my face.

"You're back!" I laugh as the other dogs run to their brothers and I am buried in a wriggling mountain of excited dogs. I sit up and rub the cheeks of Max and Mars, their eyes back to their innocent brightness.

The blackbird takes off from Grandfather Oak's branch. I hold out a hand, and he lands softly on my finger.

"Thank you, blackbird. You helped me face my fear and gave me courage. I want you to join my family, here."

The blackbird slowly shakes his head, his bright, beady eyes staring into my own.

"You don't want to stay with us?" I ask sadly.

The blackbird spreads his wings. As I stare in amazement, he begins to fade. The weight on my finger becomes lighter and lighter, until I am holding up nothing but air.

"He… He's gone!" I cry. What just happened? Was he magic? Was he even real? Confused, I scan the sky above, but there is no sign of my feathered friend.

"The blackbird is a very magical creature, Amy," Grandfather Oak says. "As a spirit guide, a blackbird will only come to those who can understand his teachings and apply them to their own lives. He came to you knowing that you doubted yourself, that you didn't have confidence in your courage. He reminded you to keep hope, even if you didn't realize it at the time."

I don't cry, and I don't grieve; I smile. My little spirit animal. I hope one day we will meet again.

I fix Mittens's head – Mr Frost and Blizzard had put it on the wrong way – and make my way to the front of my house. I take off my tiara and run my fingers through my hair.

But something catches my eye: my tiara's yellow gem – it's *glowing*! It has never glowed before!

I gently run my index finger around the edge of the jewel as Grandfather's story replays in my head.

The prince.

I look at Grandfather Oak, surrounded by the dogs and golems. He catches my eye and winks. The glow slowly fades from the gem as millions of thoughts flood my head.

Looking around, it finally hits home that things have indeed gone back to normal. My friends and family are protected from dark magic, at least for now. Tomorrow I'll get started on that doghouse, or some other building project, or I'll take another journey to explore another part of my land.

But when the sun begins to set, and we all head inside to the safety and warmth of our house, I also know that everything is not the same as before. The events of the past few days have changed me, and they've changed my view of the world.

I have so many questions, and I know my discoveries are only just beginning—

**SPLAT!**

"Mittens, cut it out!"

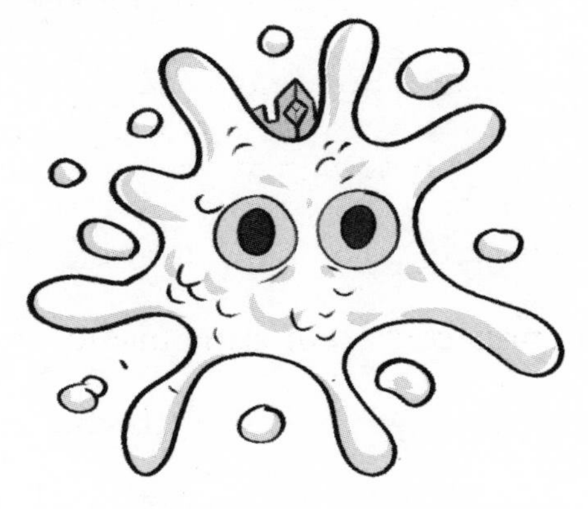

Amy Lee
X

# 10 SURPRISING FACTS ABOUT THE REAL-LIFE AMY LEE

1. I'm a vegetarian, just like my character!

2. I have a strange phobia of ostriches and wobbly teeth.

3. My favourite things other than Minecraft are Harry Potter and Pokémon!

4. I love to skateboard! My favourite boards are longboards and penny boards.

5. My favourite kind of music is heavy metal, punk and rock!

6. I still sleep with a stuffed animal!

7. In my spare time I love to draw.

8. If I wasn't a YouTuber or author, I would have been a vet or horse-riding instructor.

9. I have many clothing styles, including hippy, punk and grunge!

10. I'm very interested in the paranormal, such as ghosts and UFOs. I find it so fascinating!

# AMY LEE EXCLUSIVE INTERVIEW

## 1. AMY, WHY DID YOU START MAKING VIDEOS ABOUT MINECRAFT?

**I loved the game so much and was addicted! I had all these stories and characters in my head that I just wanted to get out and share with the world. I knew nothing about recording or editing, but with some great advice and encouragement from my YouTube friends, I was able to learn!**

## 2. IS AMY LEE THE CHARACTER DIFFERENT FROM AMY LEE THE PERSON?

We are both very similar! The only difference is the character is a lot more girly than the real-life me.

## 3. AMY HAS MANY ANIMAL FRIENDS IN THE LAND OF LOVE. DO YOU HAVE LOTS OF PETS, TOO?

Currently I have no pets. I usually have lots of animals including horses, cats, dogs, rabbits and rats, but because I travel so much I am unable to have pets right

now. Hopefully soon! I need pets in my life. Maybe I can get some puppies and name them after the doggies in the land of love!

4. WHICH CHARACTERS FROM AMY'S WORLD ARE YOUR FAVOURITES? WHAT INSPIRED YOUR CHARACTERS – FOR EXAMPLE, IS THERE A GRANDFATHER OAK IN YOUR LIFE? A PRINCE OLIVER? ;)

Mittens is one of my favourite characters. When I was in high school I was very mischievous and a prankster, so I think he is inspired by me!

Prince Oliver is inspired by someone very special. ;)

## 5.CAN YOU DESCRIBE WHAT THE PROCESS IS FOR MAKING A VIDEO? DO YOU HAVE LOTS OF HELP?

It can sometimes takes a while to get an idea for a video. I love asking subscribers for ideas on what they would like to see. I then plan it, record it and then edit. I have an editor to help when I am super busy, and sometimes I will ask my friends to help out whilst recording.

## 6. WHAT ARE YOUR FAVOURITE EPISODES THAT YOU'VE MADE?

Any episodes that are about Mittens or the Witch are my favourites. I have a lot of fun with those characters! My top favourite episode is the Halloween special in which the Witch casts a spell to make the vampire come to life from the movie. That took a very long time to record and edit, but I enjoyed it so much!

## 7. YOU HAVE LOTS OF WELL-KNOWN FRIENDS ON MINECRAFT WHO OCCASIONALLY APPEAR IN YOUR VIDEOS. HOW DID YOU GET TO KNOW THEM, AND WHAT ARE THEY REALLY LIKE?

I met Stampy and Squid three years ago after watching their videos. We all became great friends, and it felt like a real family! We've met lots of others along the way, including Mini Muka, Tomahawk, Netty Plays, Ash Dubh and many more. It's so nice having friends that do the same work, and we all support each other. I love seeing their creativity and imaginations come to life. It's also great going to conventions together; they feel like family reunions!

In real life, they are all crazy. What you see is what you get! I wouldn't change them for anything.

## 8. YOU'VE GOT LOADS OF FANS ALL OVER THE WORLD. WHAT'S IT LIKE IT BE FAMOUS?

It's a very strange experience that I was not

prepared for! I sometimes get stopped when I am out for dinner or shopping, and it blows my mind every time. My non-YouTube friends think it's hilarious. It's weird going to a store and seeing my face on a magazine!

### 9. WHAT ADVICE WOULD YOU OFFER TO KIDS WHO WANT TO START THEIR OWN YOUTUBE CHANNELS?

It's great fun! Being a YouTuber is all about sharing your love of what you do. Record what makes you happy, and let your imagination run wild!

Be safe online and never give out your personal details.

## 10. THERE CAN BE A LOT OF REALLY MEAN THINGS SAID IN THE COMMENTS SECTION ON YOUTUBE. HOW DO YOU DEAL WITH THAT KIND OF NEGATIVITY?

It's always hurtful to read such mean comments, but sadly it happens to everyone. I don't think we will ever understand why people choose to be so hurtful. You have to concentrate on the positivity and let that influence you. You can

change someone's day by what you say to them, so spread kindness.

## 11. WHAT MADE YOU DECIDE TO START WRITING BOOKS?

I have been writing stories for as long as I can remember. It has always been my dream to publish my own book. It is my dream job!

## 12. HOW DID YOU GET YOUR IDEA FOR THIS STORY?

I really wanted to develop the history of the Witch and why she

hated Amy so much. The Witch has always been full of anger, and I wanted to understand why. The story just kinda happened and wrote itself!

## 13. HOW IS WRITING A BOOK DIFFERENT FROM PREPARING EPISODES FOR YOUTUBE?

Preparing a video and writing a book starts the same way, with an idea. That's all it takes. You then explore the idea and fill in all the details. In the video, you see the weather, you see the colours, you see the background. But when writing a story, the writer has to explain everything so the reader gets a sense of the world. I find writing a lot more fun as the only limitation is your imagination, whereas in a video game there are set limitations.

## 14. WHAT ARE YOUR FAVOURITE BOOKS TO READ?

I am very inspired by JK Rowling. Harry Potter is an incredible story and her imagination is wonderful. I have read the books many times over and always

will, it's my comfort book series! Whenever I feel sad, or poorly, or just need to escape, I read Harry Potter.

## 15. IN THE BOOK, GRANDFATHER OAK TELLS AMY THAT DARKNESS AND LIGHT NEED EACH OTHER, THAT THERE NEEDS TO BE BALANCE IN THE UNIVERSE. WHAT DOES HE MEAN BY THAT?

Grandfather Oak is a very wise tree. He believes that without shadows, light cannot exist. Which is true! We also need sad times to appreciate the good times. The darkness puts all the light into perspective and teaches us more about ourselves. How we react when bad things happen shows us who we really are.

## 16. WHAT'S NEXT FOR AMY LEE? WILL THERE BE MORE BOOKS?

**Definitely! This is only the beginning!**

**Check out this other book featuring Amy Lee and her friends and family!**